Charlie and the
GREAT MASKARADE

Written by Joy Barber
Illustrated by Sarah K. Turner

"Wake up, Charlie and Tye," Mommy calls through the crack in our door.

"Today is a special day!"

Tye jumps out of his bed like a jackin-the-box. **"It's the first day of school!"** he yells.

He runs into the closet and pulls out his favorite shirt.

"I'm so excited to see my friends and meet my new teacher."

I bury my head full of curls
underneath my fluffy pillow.

"I don't want to go
to school," I grumble.

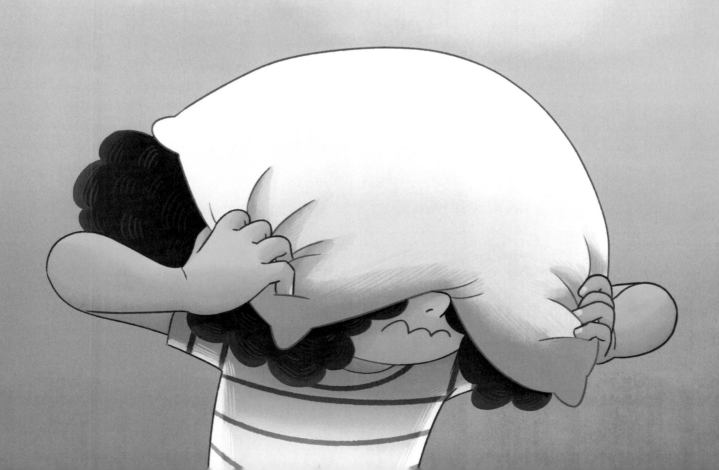

Mommy walks into our room and pulls back our curtain.
The sunlight beams through our window.

"Why don't you want to go to school, sweetheart? Aren't you excited to see your friends?"

I shake my head.

"No. There are going to be too many germs."
I close my eyes hoping to fall back asleep.

"Don't be afraid, my little superhero," Mommy says. "There's a world out there to save. By wearing a mask and washing our hands, we can fight the germs and help save the day."

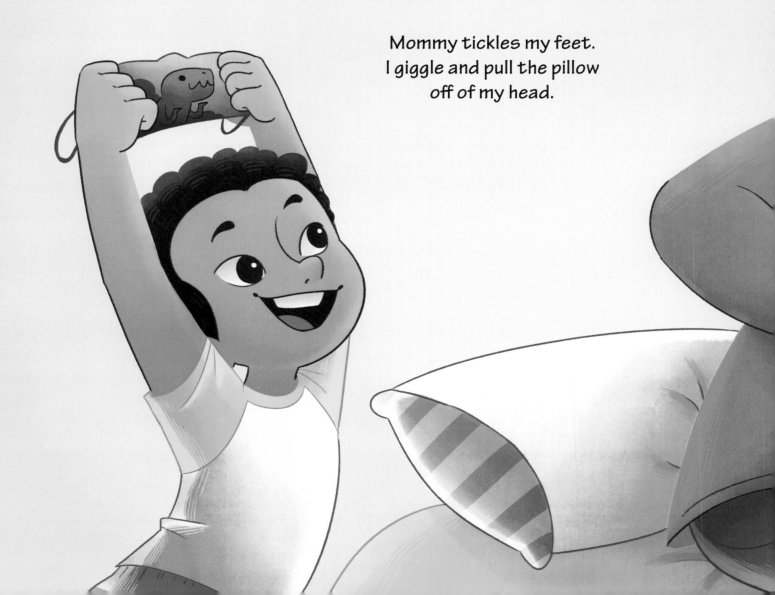

"Oooooo, I want to save the day!" Tye exclaims.

Mommy tickles my feet. I giggle and pull the pillow off of my head.

"Are you ready to help Tye save the day?" she asks.

I crawl out from under
the covers like a turtle.
"Do I have to?"

"I know you can save the
world," Mommy responds.

She kisses my forehead,
hands me a dress, and
leaves our room.

We walk to the car, and I am the last one to buckle in.
I am very quiet as we drive down the street.
Tye dances in his seat and sings at the top of his lungs.

When we arrive at the big brown school building, my stomach feels like I swallowed a million butterflies.

"Goodbye, my little superheroes!" Mommy says. "Have a great day!"

I squeeze Tye's hand as he tries to skip up the stairs.
"Tye, slow down. Aren't you scared to go in?"

"No! My mask has a big t-rex on it, and he'll bite the germs."

Uh-oh!
I touch my mask.

I don't have a dinosaur there to protect me.

When we arrive at our classroom, we meet our teacher, Mrs. Barbara. I notice she has long red hair and is wearing a colorful mask.

"Good morning, boys and girls," she says, greeting us at the front door. "Welcome to the first day of school!"

As I sit down at my
desk, I think of an idea.

I know just what to do!

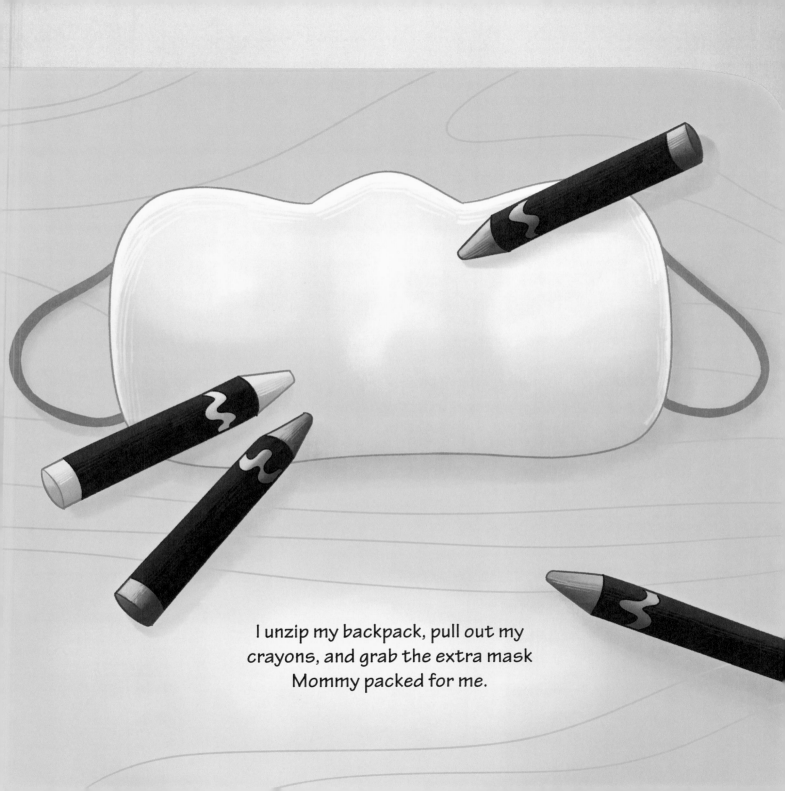

I unzip my backpack, pull out my crayons, and grab the extra mask Mommy packed for me.

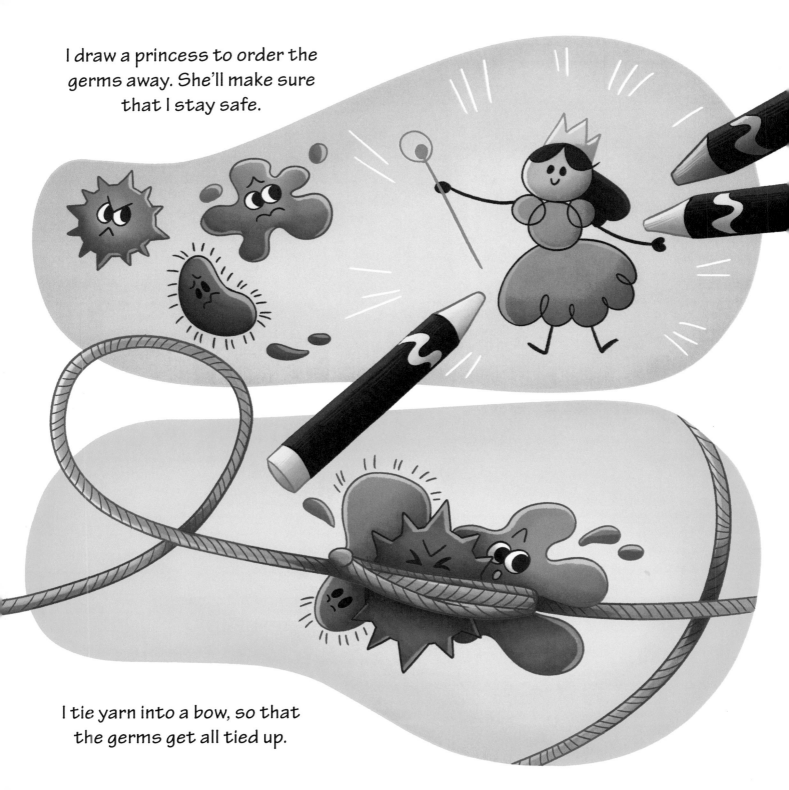

I draw a princess to order the germs away. She'll make sure that I stay safe.

I tie yarn into a bow, so that the germs get all tied up.

I add a lot of glitter to sparkle really bright, so that the germs will be blinded by the light.

I even tape tiny gummy bears from my lunchbox to growl and scare the germs.

I put on my new mask, run up to Mrs. Barbara and pull on her skirt.

I stand as tall as a tree and put my hands on my hips like a superhero.

"Oh my, Charlie...what a spectacular mask!" she exclaims.

"Thank you. I made it to help save the day."

My friends' eyes turn really big and
they start to raise their hands.

"Mrs. Barbara, I want a mask like Charlie!" a classmate shouts.

"Me too," says another.

She goes behind her desk and pulls out a package of new masks and more art supplies.

"We can all make a fantastic mask, and I have a fun surprise when everyone is finished."

Mrs. Barbara lines us up in a row towards the end of the day.

"What's the surprise?"
I raise my hand to ask.

"We're going to have a parade on the playground with everyone in their amazing new masks."

"It's a Maskarade!"
Tye shouts with glee.

"Yes, and I choose Charlie to be the Maskarade leader."

I smile so big under my mask that my cheeks begin to hurt.

I hold my head up high and lead my class around the jungle gym.

The big kids wave as they watch us march past their classroom windows.

This is the best day!

While we wait for Mommy and Daddy
to pick us up, I turn around and hug Tye.

**"I'm so glad we came to school.
We are going to have a safe
school year."**